The LOUDEST Bark

**Gail Marlene Schwartz
and Lucie Gagnon**

Illustrated by
Amélie Ayotte

At my house, everything is quiet.
My parents are quiet,
my goldfish, Bubble, is quiet,
even the doorbell is quiet.
Every sound is like a whisper.

Chloe, my new babysitter, lives across the street.
At Chloe's house, *nothing* is quiet!

Today, I am going to Chloe's house for the first time.
When she opens the door, the phone rings, a dog barks,
and funny music plays: BOOM didda BOOM didda BOOM!

A huge ball of black-and-white fur jumps on me.

"What's his name?" I ask.

"Her name is Piano, because of her colours," Chloe says.

I wish I had a dog.

Inside Chloe's house is an
explosion of colour.
"What's that?" I ask.
"Costumes. I make them for
actors in theatre and movies."

There are gazoodles of clothes everywhere:
stripy skirts, glittery gloves, poofy pants.
I touch a stretchy shirt on the sofa.
"Can I . . . "
"You want to play dress-up? Sure!" says Chloe.

"Hey, Samuel, wanna take Piano for a walk?"

"Can I go like this?"

"No, lovely one," Chloe says, "you might trip."

A few weeks later, I go back to Chloe's house.

When the door opens, I see it—the Dazzling Dress!

It's so loud, I can almost hear it sing, shout, even laugh!

"What do you think?" Chloe asks. "I just finished it
 for a new show."
I can't speak, so I nod my head fast, up and down,
up and down. I tiptoe up to the mannequin.
"You can touch it,"Chloe says.
"It's made of silk."

Bzzz!!! A sound from Chloe's phone.

"I almost forgot. Time to give Piano her vitamins," Chloe says.

"Is she sick?" I ask.

"No, didn't I tell you? Piano's going to have puppies!"

I tell Mommy and Daddy about the puppies at supper.
"Can we have one?"
"No, sweetie, we're too busy. Dogs take a lot of time
and work," Daddy says. "Want some strawberry ice cream?"
Even though it's my favourite, I shake my head and walk
slowly to my room.

That night, I dream I'm wearing the Dazzling Dress.

In my arms is a fuzzy, black-and-white puppy.

We dance, we run, then we curl up together and fall asleep.

I visit Chloe every day for the next few weeks.
With her help, I take very good care of Piano.

One afternoon, Chloe and I are singing
together in her backyard. Piano pants and
makes little whimpering sounds.

"What is it, lovely pooch?" Chloe says.
"Samuel, I think Piano might be ready to have her babies."

Chloe was right! A few hours
later, Piano is the proud
mama of four tiny puppies:
one girl and three boys.

We put different coloured ribbons around
their necks to tell them apart.
"We should give them glamorous
names like Hamlet, Zeus, or Neptune,"
Chloe says.
"How about Little Miss?" I say.
Chloe laughs. "Perfect!"

"I hope we gave the puppies the right names."

"Not sure I understand, lovely one," Chloe says.

"When I was born, the baby fairy whispered my name to my parents. They thought she said Samuel, but she really said *Simone*."

"I see. Did you tell your parents?" Chloe asks.

"Not yet."

After school, I try to play, but I'm too sad.
"What's the matter?" Mommy asks.
"Pleeeeaaase can I have a puppy?"

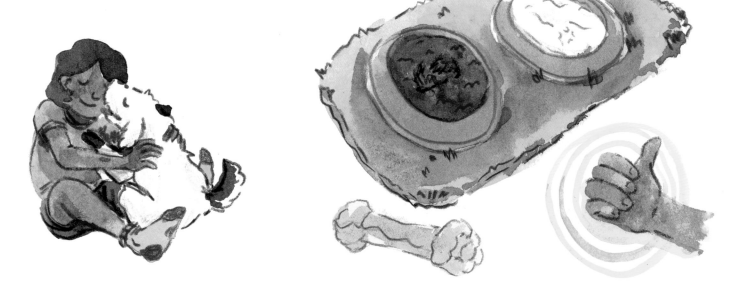

"I promise I'll take care of her, I'll feed her and give her water,
I'll brush her, and I'll walk her, I'll . . . "

"You're too young, Samuel, and besides, it's not fair to leave the dog home alone all day while we're at work and you're at school. I'm sorry, but the answer is no."

I go to my room and crawl under my desk where it's
dark and silent.
I don't want to dream about a puppy.
I don't want to dream about . . . anything at all.

On the weekend, when my parents are at the theatre, I get to have my first sleepover at Chloe's house.
Chloe opens the door and says, "Hello, Simone! Delicious to see you!"

Simone.

How wonderful that word sounds!

It's the first time someone has called me by the right name.

"Can I see the puppies?"

"Yes, but first, I have a surprise for you!" Chloe says.

Chloe gives me a box. Inside is the Dazzling Dress,
but in a smaller size. My size.

"Thanks," I whisper.

"Wanna take a walk with the dogs?" Chloe asks.

"Can I wear the dress?"

"Well, of course you can. It's yours!"

Chloe and I walk through the neighbourhood singing.

She laughs and I skip—I love how the dress flares when I twirl.

"Which puppy is your favourite, Simone?"
"It doesn't matter, my parents won't let me have one."
"Well, guess what? I spoke with your parents about that, and here's what we decided. I'm going to keep one puppy here with Piano during the week, and on weekends, it will live with you. It will be your puppy, Simone. Good idea, right?"

I run to the puppy pen and take Little Miss into my arms. The puppy licks my face and yap, yap, yaps.

"Did you pick Little Miss because she's a girl?" Chloe asks.
"No! Because she has the LOUDEST BARK!"

On our first Friday night, Little Miss sleeps, but I can't. She makes all kinds of sounds: scratches, whines, and yips. But worst of all, she snores, even louder than the giant in *Jack and the Beanstalk*.

My noisy little puppy.
I love her so much.

On Saturday, I decide to play with Little Miss in the yard. When I twirl into the kitchen in my Dazzling Dress, my parents look at each other, then smile. "Have fun with your puppy, Simone," they say.

One year later . . .

At my house, things aren't so quiet.
NOT ANYMORE!

Authors:

Gail Marlene Schwartz and Lucie Gagnon

Gail Marlene Schwartz and Lucie Gagnon are passionate about children's books. They co-authored *Clementine in Quarantine* (Facile à lire, 2020) and *My Sister's Girlfriend* (Rebel Mountain Press, 2022). Gagnon is retired from the Montreal Public Library. She is a homeschooling mom who loves games, pasta, and learning how things work. Schwartz also writes for adults and is a professional editor. She likes to sing, make challa bread, and do messy art projects with friends. Along with writing, they also share a home, a son, and a dog, all full of sound, in St-Armand, Quebec. Available for readings and school presentations. www.LuGaLit.com and www.gailmarleneschwartz.com

Illustrator: Amélie Ayotte

Amélie Ayotte is a young illustrator from Montreal, Canada. Her rampant imagination and her passion for drawing led her to study traditional animation at Cégep du Vieux Montréal. Her first short film, *Koi*, was presented at Fantasia Festival in 2018. She's studying Specialized Education at Université du Québec à Montreal, and organizes creative workshops for people of all ages. With every brushstroke, she tries to bring a bit of wonder to the world. https://amelieayotte.myportfolio.com/

The Loudest Bark
Published by Rebel Mountain Press, 2021

Library and Archives Canada Cataloguing in Publication

Title: The loudest bark / Gail Marlene Schwartz and Lucie Gagnon ; illustrations by Amélie Ayotte.
Names: Schwartz, Gail Marlene, 1966- author. | Gagnon, Lucie, 1957- author. | Ayotte, Amélie, 1998- illustrator.
Identifiers: Canadiana 20210133880 | ISBN 9781989996034 (hardcover)
Classification: LCC PS8637.C59 L68 2021 | DDC jC813/.6—dc23

Rebel Mountain Press gratefully acknowledges project support by the Province of British Columbia through the BC Arts Council.

Supported by the Province of British Columbia

Printed and bound in Canada by Marquis
ISBN 978-1-989996-03-4 (hardcover)

Rebel Mountain Press—Nanoose Bay, BC, Canada

We gratefully acknowledge that we are located on the traditional territory of the Snaw-Na-Was First Nation

www.rebelmountainpress.com

OTHER CHILDREN'S PICTURE BOOKS FROM REBEL MOUNTAIN PRESS:

Quels jappements! by Lucie Gagnon and Gail Marlene Schwartz
French language version of *The LOUDEST Bark*

COMING IN 2022:
middle-grade novels by
Gail Marlene Schwartz and Lucie Gagnon:

My Sister's Girlfriend
and
L'amoureuse de ma soeur

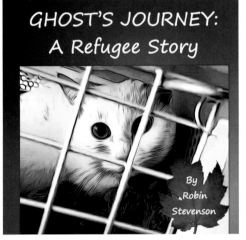

By Robin Stevenson, Illustrated by Rainer Oktovianus

When life in Indonesia becomes too dangerous for LGBTQ people, Ghost and her two dads are forced to leave their home and escape to freedom in Canada. Based on a true story, and told from the perspective of the real-life cat, Ghost.

"This introduction to LGBTQ human rights for young children is a gentle and effective one." ~***Kirkus Reviews***

Award Nominations:
2021 Silver Birch Express, and
2021 Rocky Mountain Book Award

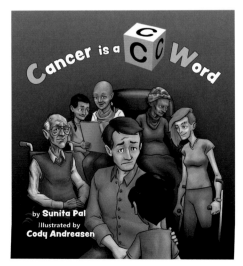

By Sunita Pal, Illustrated by Cody Andreasen

A story to help introduce the concept of cancer to children in a very simple and gentle way that is easy for them to understand. At the same time, reminding children of other stronger C words that can help someone affected by cancer, like cuddling, compassion, community, and caring.

"This gentle educational primer on a tough topic pushes through fear and lands on love." ~***Kirkus Reviews***

"Cancer is a 'C' Word invites readers to discover the many other 'C' words that support wellness. Community, Coming Together, and Caring that come alive in images that celebrate diversity."
~***Tracy Myers, Children's Counsellor***